hard unfair extraordinary weird magical awful your perception relaxing serious a joke dull yours stupid challenging unusual purposeful humbling chaotic easy short long mysterious universal harsh subjective unknown hard-work charming natural

LIFE IS ____

worthwhile authentic measurement time beautiful sincere delightful fulfilling two-faced fighting deep shallow natural death memories living motion happy sad vivid honest heartless bright changing cheerful creative full of dreams good growth honourable lifeless peaceful playful real quiet rewarding rich surprising uncommon wonderous amazing blissful breathtaking complex dynamic enchanting euphoric evolving expansive gorgeous graceful healing hopeful inspiring illuminating abrasive inhumane love gentle hateful mesmerising aggressive pleasant mortality missing witty resilient thrilling bad good unique vibrant zealous youthful brutal bitter incredible twisted sensational disappointing awesome overwhelming tiring confusing taken-for-granted constant discovery ecstatic painful horrible dazzling transcendent underappreciated passionate spiritual fluid simple tomorrow yesterday the present could be better could be worse crazy imagination experiences appreciation vision responsibility focusing energy a movie a gift story holding on transformative the past the future unforgettable hard unfair extraordinary weird magical awful your perception relaxing serious a joke dull yours stupid challenging unusual purposeful humbling chaotic easy short long mysterious universal harsh subjective unknown hard-work charming worthwhile authentic measurement time beautiful sincere delightful fulfilling two-faced fighting deep shallow natural death memories living motion happy sad natural

Also by Julia Dickerson

Stopping Time (2019)

LIFE IS ___

A compelling collection of forty short stories

JULIA DICKERSON

Follow the author on;
Instagram: @jjuliadickerson
Tik Tok: @julesdickobooks

MEMORIES, FIGHTING, PERCEPTIONS, UNKNOWN, TIME

LIFE IS ___

A compelling collection of forty short stories

ISBN: 9780648782773
Word Count: 14,095
Flesch Reading Ease: 78.5
Flesch-Kincaid Grade Level: 4.6

Publisher: Small Business Rules
9 8 7 6 5 4 3 2 1 0

The author can be contacted at jd@juliadickerson.com

DEDICATION

To those who were criticised for being themselves:
this book is for you.

"We blame society, but we *are* society"

Julia Dickerson

CONTENTS

AUTHOR'S NOTE

Thank you so much for reading my book. This book has a variety of stories, some stories I create an entire new world. And in other stories, I try to live in ours.

This book hopes to inspire people to continue to be themselves – no matter what life may throw at them.

Being normal is OK. *Not* feeling normal is OK. Being afraid is fine. Making a mistake is fine. Not achieving your goals is alright. Being behind others in the stages of life is all right. Not feeling like yourself every day is normal.

What matters is that you don't change *who you are*. Don't change your spark. Don't change your weird and funny remarks. Don't change your true hobbies. Don't change your positivity. I know it is hard, but who are you if not yourself?

Growing and maturing out of these things is OK and changing habits is OK, but only if it is what *you* want and not what others have told you to do. And if you do change, that is OK too. But don't wish you were your 'old self' or 'someone else' if you've grown as a person.

This is your life. Your world. So, make sure that it is yours.

Sometimes we feel like we don't touch the lives of other people. Or we feel like our personality is never truly shown to everyone. It is. It truly is. No matter the mood you are in, your aura will truly reflect your personality. I have attached letters from 15 different people that were addressed to me over my life.

I hope this inspires you to continue to be yourself.

★   "What makes you so special is that you are not afraid to be you. When we are all born, we don't know that we are meant to conform to society's version of normal. We just cry when we want food and poop when we feel like it. Unfortunately, somewhere along the way, we start to 'learn' that we must be similar to everyone else in order to fit in. and the individual characteristics that make us all so special start to be lost and people start to look like sheep. Except you. Not only do I gain a sense that you are incredibly proud to be you, but I feel that you are strong enough as an individual to always believe in yourself and always be yourself. I just can't see you being convinced by society to conform to the accepted version of what a person should be like or what a person should do. Keep in mind there are probably some aspects of conformity that might need to be adhered to. Not running a red light, not murdering someone because they stole your cool trackies, that type of thing. But in terms of behaviour and who you are, I am incredibly proud of your strong sense of who you are and your conviction of how you go about this complicated process of living. I never want you to lose that unique sense of you. I know it seems obvious, but don't lose this positive attitude that you carry with you at all times. You have had some setbacks in life – some minor and some major – but you have maintained a very positive attitude despite those setbacks. Life can throw some pretty interesting curveballs at you but I believe that you are well-equipped to deal with them. Whatever you do, it will be special, unique, fantastic and will bring joy to those who come near the aura that is JED."

★ "…You can make decisions and everyone seems to follow you. Your ability to lead without being bossy is a wonderful trait to have as it is done in such a positive way. Perhaps it is this ability that has helped you while you have been sick. You have just gone along with all the doctor appointments (and we have been to lots!) and have not complained…It is what it is and at the moment there doesn't seem to be a magical fix so you keep going and doing your thing. And even with this illness you are still going so well at school. You are such a kind and happy soul. You come up with so many different ideas and love doing your own thing. You deserve fabulous things to happen for you."

★ "I'm sure that no matter what you pick to end up doing you will do well at it, just make sure you push yourself to the absolute limit all the time."

★ "I mean this with all my heart that you are the most deserving, amazing, positive, lovely and happy girl I know. Your kind heart and beautiful smile never fails to make my day and I know whenever I see you, even if it may not be often, that we will have a blast. I have learnt so much from you and we have been through so much together…Never forget who you are; a beautiful, intelligent, happy, hilarious human being."

★ "You have always been so true to yourself, not scared to be different which I so admire. Also, you get so involved in life which makes it so fun to spend time with you. Never ever change because you are elite."

★ "You have always been there for me without you or me even noticing it. You are truly inspirational – I love it! Just you being you is all you need…yourself!"

★ "It has been my extreme fortune, joy and supreme honour to be in your life. You have already proven how strong and adaptable you can be and I am excited for your continued amazing-ness!"

★ "Thank you for being such an amazing, funny and friendly person in my life who never fails to brighten my day. You're so random and I love your craziness. I've enjoyed every moment I've spent around you. Your bubbly personality is like no other and although you're one of the weirdest people I've ever met, you're one of the best."

★ "I admire your ability to light up a room with your charisma and smile."

★ "I love that you're uniquely yourself. You have such a vibrant energy. Can also put a smile on my face."

★ "You never shy away from a challenge or an opportunity to express yourself. Keep shining and following your dreams."

★ "I like your ability to show passion in what you're doing and having the confidence to pursue your interests."

★ "You are such a vibrant and amazing person. I wish I was as strong and kind hearted as yourself."

★ "I love your bubbly energy that lights up a room and the ability to put a smile on people's faces."

★ "You have already seen in your life that it is not always fair, and yet, you have learnt to overcome these obstacles with great resilience and determination. The way that you have maintained a positive outlook is a lesson to us all, and will set you in good stead for the rest of your life."

LIFE IS <u>MEMORIES</u>

MEMORIES

Memories are a way of telling how much time has passed.

A way of holding onto your own truth, the malleability of the past.

It turns out that memories are similar to dreams.

The line becoming blurred between imagination and the reality stream.

And once we realise that our memories are flawed completely, we demand an explanation;

Why? Why are our lives a lie? Why do our past events twist and turn each other around without hesitation?

We can't trust our memories wholly, which makes us question if we can even trust anything.

And if we can't even do this, then what is the truth of everything?

★ ★ ★

SHATTERED ILLUSIONS

The room bears witness to an unsettling amount of blood, a silent testament to the wounds inflicted upon our connection. You, once a prominent figure in my life, have vanished from view, leaving me to grapple with the echoes of your absence.

Layer by layer, you peeled back the complexities of my being, delving into the depths that others merely grazed. I believed you knew me, or at least, I desperately wanted you to. In the recesses of my mind, I yearned for you to comprehend the high regard with which I spoke of you, unaware of the contrasting narrative that unfolded behind closed doors.

Yet, another cut, sharp and profound, severed the illusions I held dear. You occupied the top tier of my priorities, while I rotted in the shadows of yours. The person I thought mirrored my essence, thriving on the joy of a shared soul, was nothing but an illusion.

You stand a metaphorical mile away, distant and elusive. Even now, I strain to see you, realising that perhaps I never truly did.

The world, with its relentless changes, conspired to pull us apart. You became a fleeting presence in my life, a mere glimpse that failed to evolve into a lasting connection.

The pain runs deep, the cuts profound. It hurts to give so much of oneself, only to discover that the reciprocity is absent. You, oblivious to the sacrifices and investments made on your behalf, remain a distant silhouette. The realisation stings - the person I held in such high regard failed to see me.

Attempting to revisit what shattered us is worthless. The shards are irreparable, and attempting to piece them back together would only inflict more damage. It is a stark truth that one cannot return to what broke them; the attempt only worsens the fractures, leaving scars that linger as reminders of a connection that once held great promise. And so, I stand in the aftermath, nursing wounds that time alone can heal, vowing to tread forward, stronger and wiser, towards a future untouched by the pain of shattered illusions.

GO

Please.

Stay.

No. Leave.

I wonder if there is more to say.

Why did it all just drift away?

I used to see your face in every crowd.

Now, your photos feel cold.

The bond we shared.

It can't be for nothing.

I wonder if there is still time.

Time to change the hurt.

Wait. Stay.

No. Please leave me.

Goodbye.

Now read it from the bottom to top.

SORRY

I know you hate that you will never get the apology that you deserve, so I'm going to be the one to apologise to you. I'm sorry that you trusted the wrong person. I'm sorry that you miss the 'old' you. I'm sorry that you believed that they deserved better, but you were the one that deserved that. I'm sorry that you spent countless nights crying over the way that you felt, when everyone else had no idea. I'm sorry that you feel so lost and are just counting the hours away to go to sleep. I'm sorry that you can't trust people easily now. I'm sorry that no one ever made you feel like yourself and the ones that did, ran away. I'm sorry you hate the way your body feels and the way you speak to yourself. I'm sorry that they had no idea of the way you felt and words felt like nothing.

I'm sorry. I'm sorry for all of it. You deserved better.

FORGOTTEN LANGUAGES

Handwritten letters from your childhood best friend. Patience. Dancing until midnight. A text from your old high school group. Reading old birthday cards you saved every year. Giving people another chance. "Are you okay?" Talking for hours. Surprising your parents. Driving and singing by yourself. Double texting. "I'll save you a seat." Remembering the little things. Nicknames. Listening to an old voicemail. First impressions. Someone telling you their favourite memory of you. Caring too much. Apologies. Snuggling next to your teddy bear. People listening to you without speaking. Someone organising to hang out with you and all you have to do is show up. Crying together. Making the first move. Someone playing a song because they thought you would like it. Standing up for your friend. Your dog loving your friends. Having the same amount of care and love for each other. Forgiveness. Smiling across the room. Surprises. "Text me when you get home safely." Watering your plant when you're not there. Texting straight away. "This reminded me of you." Flowers.

★ ★ ★

INSEPARABLE TO NON-EXISTENT

I really pictured this year differently.

I pictured us moving out together at the end of the year - all three of us. The trio that was always inseparable. The trio where we've all seen each other at our worst. We had cried in front of each other. We knew how to trigger each other and push each other's buttons. We had spent every single day together. We brought out the best in each other. All three of us.

Then one day it all fell apart.

But the thing is though, I didn't do anything.

We didn't have an argument.

None of us made a massive mistake.

We had all seen each other recently and everything was fine.

Why did you both say then that you wanted nothing to do with me? Why?

If I had done something horribly, at least I would be able to learn and grow from my actions and understand why you did and say what you did.

But I did absolutely nothing wrong.

I just don't understand. And I wish I could.

I guess we really didn't bring out the best in each other. I guess I shouldn't have been as comfortable around you as I was. I guess we were separable.

You're now blacklisted from everything associated with me.

I think losing friends that meant the world to you is the hardest thing to move on from.

Especially when they were your whole world.

YESTERDAYS

It's strange to think that I most likely remember today.

I won't remember the hurried dash to class or the sensation of being drenched in the pouring rain.

Tomorrow will be the same. It will join the long list of yesterdays. Blending seamlessly into one another. Memories are peculiar. They capture moments we cherish and others we yearn to escape.

Everything is temporary. Life is temporary. Pain is temporary. Amidst the nature of life's experiences going, there is at least comfort knowing that pain will eventually fade. Sometimes, yes, we do want to remember. But sometimes, we also just want to forget.

As I walked through my hometown, a sense of nostalgia crept in. The city I had called home had seen countless sunsets and sunrises, each day blending into the next. Yet, every day seemed slightly different, even if most of them would fade away.

Looking around, the world still continued to move. Even though I stayed still. A reminder that life is made up of countless memories, each in their own way. Today might become another forgotten memory, but it is a part of the chapter in your story, unfolding, each moment at a time.

MEMORY'S MELODY

The hum of existence reverberated around me, a constant reminder that change was the only true constant. Life unfolded in its own rhythm, sweeping everyone along in its relentless current.

Unexpectedly, disruption struck, casting chaos into this routine. A stranger, a mere silhouette against the canvas of my life, emerged in the face of adversity. In that moment, we became allies in dealing with this disruption, our shared struggles removing the barriers of unfamiliarity.

The highs and lows, painted the tapestry of our intertwined lives. Happiness found its significance in contrast to the lows, turning ordinary moments into extraordinary ones. It was the acknowledgment that without the depths of despair, joy wouldn't shine as brightly.

As time flowed, the invisible force shaping our destinies, memory played its subtle yet profound role. The echoes of shared experiences lingered between us, forming the foundation of our connection. Even amidst the chaos, there was a certain rhythm in the recollection of moments that bound us together.

Life, I realised, wasn't just about the mechanical routine. It was about shared experiences, unity in facing adversity, and the understanding that joy and pain were intertwined, etched into the fabric of our memories. The world might whisper about its impending end, but in the dance of existence, memory became the thread that wove a narrative, urging us to navigate the ever-changing landscape together.

LIFE IS FIGHTING

THE END OF MAN IS NEAR

The silent whispers of a puny inexhaustible voice tell me that I cannot escape. It declares my inevitable entrapment. They tickle the outside of my ear and become a white noise that will not give up, swirling around me like a maddening chorus.

"The end of man is near. The end of man is near."

The darkness covering my eyes is slowly filled with an influx of colour. The void shrouding my vision and pulsating with thick vibrance of hues, each more vivid than the last. Guns are screaming, the cacophony of warring weapons drowning out the voices, rendering it powerless. My tinnitus reactivates and ignites, unleashing a piercing screech that shakes my very core.

It is time.

Time for what? The inextricable power that forcibly sinks my heart every time I wake up, suffocating me? The seemingly endless loop that replays every time I open my eyes? The fact that the base of everything is to be afraid and I am just scraping the bottom at the moment? And all I am is but a mere speck in its shadow?

It is the same movement every day. The same actions from those surrounding me. Mechanical. Monotonous. And the same results at the end of every day.

I move the mass of my body to the edge of my mattress. Sitting up, I feel that I am stuck in an endless black void silently screaming for help. My voice shrinking to nothing. My body being dragged towards the brink of oblivion.

In an automated movement, I grab my 20kg bergen and attach it to my back after dressing myself in identical clothing to all the others. I feel suspended in a bottomless pit, my silent screams for help becoming swallowed. And as I walk out of our shelter, I question, "When will it be my time?"

WHAT'S CONSIDERED NORMAL?

When you're not perceived to be 'normal' or able to do 'normal' things, you will literally scream in silence, begging the universe for one day of freedom. Even just one hour. You're being exerted on by a force bigger than the universe's power and trapped under a boulder, even Sisyphus can't roll. And you beg, and beg for even one minute.

And nobody will ever be able to truly understand you, no matter how much you voice. But, what you hope, is that someone is there that cares enough to try.

And to the naked eye, you're fine. To the naked eye, your voice is heard. To the naked eye, you're 'normal'. But give that eye a glimpse of clothing and it will be blinded.

But while you're begging to be considered 'normal'…maybe you already are.

Maybe all of our definitions of 'normal' is different, and maybe normal is a word that has no real meaning behind it.

Maybe while you're pleading to feel normal, others are pleading to feel the way you do.

Maybe the way everyone is, is exactly where and who we are meant to be.

ANGER, PAIN, FORGET…REPEAT

"If you fall, that's the end", they said.

Destroying humanity as we fled.

Stripped of our clothing in the cold,

Antisemitism was the reason, we were told.

We were deprived of socialisation

through brutal dehumanisation.

Shoved raspingly and pushed around,

Hunting humans, everyone to be found.

Anger led to brutal eradication,

One dictator, fearful of liberation.

And *still* we walked through the snow,

Fleeing a camp, so no one would know.

Why did one man change the course of history?

Hate, anger, fear...it all remains a mystery.

He had copious anger bottled inside,

Deeming us insignificant, sent to the outside.

Looking back, all walked away broken,

Hiding themselves, their feelings unspoken.

Six million lives were illicitly removed,

But *still* today, these actions have to be proven.

History is beginning to repeat itself,

Books full of records, buried on every shelf.

All of us have tried to forget,

Begging, *pleading*, not to hit reset.

We have to remember, so you never do,

Our memories should be the *only* preview

of the effect caused by the human condition.

Firstly struck at the most powerful, coming to fruition.

They were unprepared for our arrival

the first time - forced into survival.

If these actions replicate again,

They'll be ready, *their* hatred leading to *your* pain.

Anger leads to fear, hate, then mass execution,

Stop it...please find a solution.

WHITE NOISE

The large statue boomed, with the relaxation coming upon strangers. The inextricable connection all felt towards Big Ben – at first the fear of *another* loud noise being silenced by the monotonous tone. People were turning to hibernation, to hide and stay until the deaths stopped. Dust covered the sky and the white noise drowned life into a positive warfare. The sky became blue-less as the clouds reflected our city. The roads turned into a suicide mission as the people were hunted. Barriers, weapons and fear became our internal and external suit as the corruption took place.

"Mrs. Croft?", whispered a small child.

"Clarence…hide! You can't be seen in public," I harshly stated. We can't have children fearful of the future from the war. We have to save a generation.

As Clarence ran away, wind drained our energy as temporary houses began flying and our barriers became loose. The force was pushing me one way as I ran to the other. Big Ben struck again as the white noise disappeared. Shouts from leaders overlapped. My hair blew across my face. I was unable to see as I moved, my sensory images becoming overloaded.

The fighters ran out, as the young men, laughing girls, the shopkeepers…everyone hid.

Clarence was hiding in the latch under a building. An unforeseeable object that had a glimmer of light through a tiny crack. We hid together.

We watched…and we waited…countless strikes from the tower made us become weary and helpless. Death filled our eyes, mouth and ears. Crying helpless people.

Through the tiny horizontal crack, I made eye contact with a nice boy I've known for three years. His family used to make me dinner when I was alone. The reminiscent smells of a crispy cooked chicken filled with spice and their special blend of herbs filled my nose as I stared at him.

As I took a deep breath in, smells of blood and mud filled my lungs and the boy was on the ground.

I began to rush out the latch as Clarence grabbed my hand and whispered, "Don't".

I was frozen. A still, life-less body lay still, staring at me.

He was there! He was still there!

But that interior disappeared…I don't understand.

When, and *how*, will this end? Why?

★ ★ ★

A DANCE WITH THE DEMONS

A cage without bars, a prison within the mind;

Trapped by the thoughts which are unkind.

The weight of regret forced like a boulder on the soul;

A never-ending cycle, an endless toll.

A dance with the demons, a twisted, dark waltz;

In the solitude of the mind where the memories assault.

The laugher, the love, the memories now lost;

Replaced by the emptiness, but at what cost?

The darkness creeps in with a suffocating shroud;

A life lived in shadows and no sun to be found.

An endless nightmare, a never-ending night;

A prison of the mind, with no end in sight.

But within the depths of the soul there's a flicker of hope;

A spark of resilience which helps us cope.

A voice whispers softly, reminding us of the light;

Guiding us towards the truth and away from the night.

So, we rise, like the Phoenix from the fire;

Reborn with a strength that no challenge can tire.

A new day begins with a heart full of grace;

And we leave behind the prison, the emptiness, this place.

WE ARE TRAPPED

It is trapped.

My core.

It holds the darkness within and encloses it tightly.

I used to be completely filled with darkness.

But something overcame me.

I am dripping away.

Leisurely releasing the darkness that has been trapped inside of me.

And exposing it into the world.

All around me, my core lies there. Still. Not moving. With the silence of the waves and crashes of my darkness unleashing itself.

Above me, in the sky, my core has been extricated into the Earth and harmed thousands.

I am dripping away.

What trapped me?

The force that held me captive lacked the strength to expel the darkness reflected within me. It wasn't strong enough to force out the evil within.

As the horizon unfolds across my world, my inner darkness significantly diminishes, freeing itself from within me to connect with humanity.

I am dripping away.

There are forces so intoxicating in this world, that none of us can escape from it.

We are trapped.

In this world and in this life.

I have now set you free.

Use it wisely.

I HATE AND I LOVE

I hate these scars.

I hate that I have to heal from something that isn't my fault.

I hate how damaged I am but I can't change anything.

I hate how this is all out of my control.

I hate that I give so much but get nothing in return.

I hate that I have to take a pill for the rest of my life to want to be here.

But I love the strength from my wounds.

I love the moments of peace in the midst of chaos.

I love the support of those surrounding me.

I love the possibility of a future where I am not haunted by the shadows of my past.

I love the small victories in my journey.

I love the compassion that I have for others.

I love the hope that whispers in the quiet moments.

But I love the beauty that emerges from the brokenness of our world and ourselves.

LIFE ISN'T FAIR

Life isn't fair.

Nothing is fair.

Being sick isn't fair.

Having mental and physical problems isn't fair.

Being misunderstood isn't fair.

The meaningless words they said isn't fair.

Having dreams shattered isn't fair.

Struggling with self-doubt and self-esteem isn't fair.

Facing rejection isn't fair.

Losing a loved one isn't fair.

Living in poverty isn't fair.

Experiencing betrayal isn't fair.

Suffering the consequences of other's actions isn't fair.

People forgetting all of the good you have done isn't fair.

Fighting silent battles isn't fair.

Being judged for factors beyond your control isn't fair.

The unpredictability of life isn't fair.

Living in fear isn't fair.

Feeling lonely in a crowded room isn't fair.

Life isn't fair.

But we all have fleeting moments of unfairness in our lives. This doesn't make it right to think less of someone else's situation. Or judge them based on their situation.

Life isn't fair.

But what matters is that you don't change yourself in the process of life to be someone you're not.

LIFE IS <u>YOUR PERCEPTION</u>

PERCEPTIONS

The most powerful and different place anyone has ever been to is their own mind. You live inside your own head your entire life - so make it an interesting place to stay. Everyone's mind continually changes over time and can differ how they react to real-life situations. No-one's mind is like anyone else's - it is all about perception. The way that someone perceives something is completely and utterly different to something else. The way that colour is perceived is different - we all call, 'blue', the same, but we all see, 'blue', divergently. Our own mind is the most striking and intoxicating location luring us in.

DROWNING

He tossed and turned in his bed, the silence screaming at him. He reached out in the endless sea of sheets, but found nothing. He turned around in his head, his consciousness flipping over and over at him - a ubiquitous and unexplained phenomenon that suffocated him. He's drowning.

An unfathomable stream of thoughts bounced from life to death situations. Stay or go? He *could* listen to his own heartbeat and drive the uncertainty away to finally be free...Or engulf his gut and listen to rationality. Which voice would he drown completely?

And as he closed one door, another door, one that was more significant, more consequential and more powerful, would unlatch. Each new door stating, 'fight' or 'flight'. This eternal Battle Royale between himself, his mind, his body and the devil following him haunted him. This demon telling him that this was just a gamble, a scheme and scam to say that it was all a waste - *everything* was for nothing.

His enemy mirrored himself. Stuck in his indecisiveness and pain.

And the only thing that stopped him from a decision was himself.

Every step he took. Every movement made. All led upstream to another door. Each door ready to wash his life away. 'Pick up your feet, that's all you have to do', voiced another door - far from him.

One last fight before he left.

The last hint of reality streamed out in front of him, a new battle in every corner.

His mind jumped over obstacles. Pushing away the fears and doubt that choked him.

He listened to that one lone voice. The voiceless figure in the shadows. Telling him to fight once more before freedom. Before releasing the demon.

He's free.

★ ★ ★

A STEP BACK

You never realise how horribly someone treated you until you take a step back and look at it all. They didn't even have the respect to talk to you about it in person. They didn't even have the decency to say it when they were sober. They didn't even have the guts to say that you didn't even cause any of this – it was someone else all along. You should have left a long, long time ago. What even makes you stay at this point? For the hopes that they would become someone that they never want to be?

"We need a serious chat."

"I haven't had fun in weeks because of you."

"You need to drink to have fun."

"You are killing me."

"I'm freaking out."

"I have to go to hospital because of you."

"I hope you die."

"I can't believe you don't see this."

"What's done is done."

"I'm fine."

"I have been living in fear because of what you have done."

"I'm getting blind."

"Why aren't you drinking?"

"I hope we are still chill!!"

And after all of that, why do we still give them so many excuses for their actions? *It is just who they are, they've just had a hard day, they just do this to everyone, it's not you, you're just over-reacting.*

It's *just* this. It's *just* that.

It should have *just* been the end after the first incident.

WE ARE ILLUSIONS

Everything is an illusion.

And we are all a part of that.

You cannot forget and leave your past behind. No matter how hard you try, the effect it had on you and other people will always be there.

We are all just an illusion.

The tightness of the cloth bag around my neck is still lingering in my body with the tape still covering my mouth slightly. The ropes are compressing deeper and deeper into my skin and struggling to release blood flow to my hands and feet. The quiet whimpers of thousands of other female voices - fighting to be heard.

We are here alone.

I drag myself harshly towards a wall and bang my body against it. I reach my feet for the wall and kick and kick and kick.

I hear people outside.

I hear voices.

I hear males.

And we are all left trapped inside.

These voices are left trapped.

Because of him.

How are we able to see everything? Eyes were created to be able to see the world.

But we are all living in an illusion, a creation where nothing is real.

Where living is not real.

We are all just an illusion.

I'm staring at my brother and my air flow is becoming cut off and trapped. His eyes glaring at mine. Liquid being created in his eyes and trying to blink it away. Eyebrows and mouth twitching slightly, trying to hold back a thousand sobs. His viridescent eyes were fading as the ground meets with the green in his eyes and the warmth arises in his cheeks.

The quiet whimpers of thousands of other female voices are screaming in my head.

He was like a father to us.

I step forward, and place my arms around him, creating warmth for both my brother and I. I hold him tightly and begin heaving and screaming - liquid pouring everywhere.

"He is gone," they said.

And as I continue pour my heart to my brother, he wipes the green away in his eyes and has no more emotion.

I am here alone.

I reach for my brother's hand but he continues to push me away and away and away.

I hear males.

But I never hear females.

All of these voices trapped inside, struggling to speak.

We are trapped.

Because of him.

Every component. Every word. Every sound.

We are all trapped inside this illusion, with no escape.

We are all just an illusion.

As my legs move onto the stage and I stare at the audience, their eyes are drifting away. My legs move leisurely towards the grand structure centred in the stage. Pitch black, with a row of pure ivory keys shimmering in the light.

I take my seat, adjusting it to my height, and place the beige sheet in front of my eyes. I pick up the weight of my hands, shaking gently, and place it carefully on the keys. Pressing the first key, the hammer hits the string and thousands of other steel strings vibrate together as the symphony flows out from me. It creates a powerful mellow sound resonating through every ear in the audience.

My gaze turns toward the front of the stage, they are all staring at me. They are looking at my hand placement, the posture of my back, to see if I missed a note. They are judging me for me, and not for my sound.

The whimpers of every voice are screaming at me inside.

To leave.

But I am here alone.

I struggle to continue making my hands move but I have to keep pushing and pushing and pushing.

I hear people clapping.

I hear voices.

I hear men.

But not clapping for my sound.

Not clapping for the performance I just created.

Clapping for the way I appeared on stage. For every detail I had perfected.

As the next competitor stepped into the spotlight and took his seat, all eyes were fixed upon them.

But they were waiting for his sound, they were waiting.

They listened. To him.

But not to me.

And I feel so trapped inside and I am struggling to break free.

Because of him.

Nothing ends when the sun sets or starts when the sun rises.

It is the same as the day before.

We are all just an illusion.

I twist my feet into the pedals and lock them in place. Gazing around, thousands of females and males have gathered to compete. I tighten my helmet around my neck and grip the handlebars tightly, waiting for the countdown. As the loud speakers say 'go', my hair whips back as my legs begin the motion of going around and around and around. Spokes turn to a blur as we begin to go faster, and it becomes one. My head remains focussed in front of me, pedalling all of my strength out.

As I gaze to my left, he is staring at me.

I quickly snap my head back to the centre and instantly have embarrassed, worried and disgust about to verbally vomit up on myself.

I want to scream at him, with millions of whimpers of voices all exasperated for ruining my race.

He made me cower and struggle in my own skin.

He beat me in the race.

Everyone cheered for him, and not for me.

And I feel trapped inside my own skin.

Because of him.

We are all interrelated in a never-ending circle.

Yesterday, today and tomorrow are a part of this circle.

We trust that time is linear and continues forever.

And we can never leave anything behind.

We are all just an illusion.

One foot in front of another. Placing a heavy weight after a heavy weight. Holding my handbag tightly in one hand and my coffee in the other. Rushing off to my workplace where I feel safe and not trapped in my own mind. The wind gushes through my hair which makes me lose focus and trip over myself. A person suddenly reaches their hand out to help catch me.

It is all an illusion.

I look up and see that a male is offering his hand. He looks genuinely concerned for me and he is trying to speak to me.

Voices. Male voices.

But I am zoning out.

I pat down my hair, take a sip of my coffee and he asks if I am okay.

Men are an illusion.

I brush off the comment and he asks where I am going so he can walk with me.

He seems kind.

And he walks me to my work and we talk and talk and talk.

He seems kind.

Our eyes play this illusion on us.

Do not trust it.

Every voice is screaming and struggling inside of me.

I feel powerless around him.

And he thinks that he has control over me.

I am trapped.

And so is every other female.

We are trapped in our own mind.

Because of him.

You can never leave what the past did to you behind.

It will struggle with you forever.

But everything you see, everything you feel and hear, is all interrelated.

We are all illusions.

FEAR

Internally, everyone is the same.

Externally, we all try and change ourselves.

What is the difference?

I was wide awake at this point, lying perfectly at ease. Pressed firmly against the headboard, my head strained to reach the snooze button on my watch. The curly brown dog lay still, a constant white noise, that made the room fill with peace. We were both perfectly still at that point in time.

Entire conversations exist only within my mind - a battle within myself. Everything I see or read, springs my mind with ideas - one going positively and the other negatively. Like two opposite devils on either shoulder. You never know which voice to listen to when they're all yours.

I grab my watch, sitting on the edge of my bed, stretching my head towards the roof in a fatigued tone. I stretched, and cracked my body, preparing myself for the day. The dog looks more exhausted than me - which he shouldn't, considering he sleeps all day. Preparing myself for another day externally, and internally - for that battle within myself.

Every time a ringing noise occurs, my whole brain shuts down. Like one voice is trying to overtake the other. It always happens in the left ear, and when it happens, I find myself at a standstill amongst constant motion. A barrier between the world and I.

I scrunch my face, splash water to wake me up and stand in the bathroom - still in time. I'm not saying anything verbally, but my voice inside isn't terminating. I think I fear my own voice. I fear what can happen if I stop talking on the inside. I'm scared of myself.

My internal voice constantly fights. Like two people are stuck within my head and are fighting to the death. I am scared what is going to happen if one does destroy the other. I fear my own internal self.

I fear myself.

★ ★ ★

MOMENTS

It still never goes away.

You will still have your good moments and your happy moments but it is still always there.

And it does not matter who you are with or where you are at or what stage of life, there is still always a hole that you cannot fill.

And that is so scary.

That you will never be content in your own life. Still always searching for something more that will never, ever come.

And you cannot wait until life is not hard anymore to decide that you can be happy – because it always will be.

Scary.

THINGS TO LOOK FORWARD TO

Moving into a new house with your best friends. Driving by yourself listening to Jungle's new album. Getting home and seeing your dog. Seeing a friend that you haven't seen in 2 years, and it's still the same. Friday nights. Laughing with your friend over a weird noise they made. Seeing your family for Christmas. Taylor Swift. Reading a poem someone wrote you. Tomorrow. Flowers that you bought yourself. Getting promoted. Wakeboarding in New Zealand with your friends. Speaking to someone for the first time, who turns out to be your best friend. Growing old with your friends. Falling over and laughing about it. Getting your first real pay check. Having a massage. Going sky-diving for the first time. Waking up and having breakfast ready for you. Hearing your old school song and still remembering the dance moves for it. Clear skin. Sticking to your new good habits. Failing, and learning. Playing your old instrument again. Completing your bucket list. Waking up without your alarm. Watching a sunset. Owning a Pollock painting. Decorating your own room. Seeing your first White Christmas. Going fruit-picking for strawberries. Receiving a hand-written letter. Using a journal small enough to carry in your purse. Walking through a secret passage. Resting on the couch watching Red Dog for the 10th time. Being yourself.

YOU

Have you ever wondered why you'd dislike yourself? I mean, think about it. You're the only one who knows which part of your hand gets all inky when you write stuff down. And who else is aware of that one tooth that protests when you chomp into something cold?

Look in the mirror, and you'll see more than just brown or green eyes staring back at you. It's a mix of both, a secret colour blend that's uniquely yours. And when you're alone, do you notice how you tend to chat and argue with yourself more than you would with others around?

Think about it. You're the only one who's been through all the ups and downs, seen the world through your own eyes. Remember holding the umbrella dead centre over your head to keep the rain off your hair? Yep, that was all you.

You're the one doing all the thinking and figuring out. So, with all that in mind, why would you ever hate yourself? You're pretty much the expert on you. Own it.

LIFE IS <u>UNKNOWN</u>

THE UNKNOWN

Dots of blackness covered my eyes. Little specks that bounced awake when my head started crumbling. Invisible to others but ever so present to me.

But, nothing is allowed to pause when this happens. Life continues moving on. Even though these dots arrive every two weeks, I am not allowed to stop.

Blind spots. Flashing lights. Zigzagging lights. Nausea. Sensitivity to the world. Fatigue. Weakness in my body.

All invisible.

I just wished I could see the world like everyone else does.

Everyone has always wished to be an only child. But I have always wished for what they have. They always come complaining to me about their siblings, and whenever I go home, it's empty. It is nice by myself, but sometimes I wished I had someone to always talk to.

And, of course, this would change how I act and who I am compared to people who have siblings.

I just wished I could see the world like everyone else does.

This sudden burst of energy makes everything feel like a video game. Like I'm a detective on the hunt for the murderer. It's given me purpose this mission. Normal people's glances make me think that they are guilty. A simple flick of an eyelid determines my thoughts about them. I am out of breath chasing people around, searching. I'm on top of the world.

In the moment, I can't tell that I've just gone downtown for a coffee. It's like my mind has fun twisting and turning the narrative in front of my eyes.

And then, this high dropped to a horrible low. I'm stuck in my bed for the past three days. I feel worthless. I don't want to eat. I'm feeling guilty from nothing I've actually done.

And everyone just says get up. Get out of bed. I physically cannot. I hate the world.

I just wished I could see the world like everyone else does.

I would always wish for something different. I would wish to not have this constant worry that I've pushed myself too hard. Or wish that I wouldn't be out of breath from walking up three stairs. Or that I wouldn't feel sharp pain in areas of my body that anyone else my age wouldn't feel. Or that my family would constantly be worried about me, as if I was a thin slate of ice. I just wished that things would be different.

I would often wonder how much of my life would be different if I didn't have this constant void attached to me.

But I just wish that things could be different. I wish I wasn't this way.

I just wished I could see the world like everyone else does.

Not a single person has or will ever see the world the same. Your 'illness' doesn't define you, but provides a large aspect of your perception of the world. When you stare at someone else, it is impossible to be able to grasp all of the experiences, emotions and perspectives that have. And, you will never be able to understand it fully and completely either. Wishing for something and someone that isn't you is not possible. And it isn't fair to you.

No one is the same as you.

Yes, some would say this perhaps this 'void' has changed you, but maybe this was where you were meant to be all along.

WHEN THE WORLD GOES BLANK

I was always told to ask the questions rather than to answer them...

As the lid closes above me, my eyes instinctively shut, and the soft click of the door's lock resonates, accompanied by the symphony of a million other locks filling my ears. I am not alone in this confined space; the awareness is shared among us all.

A coldness fills my body – beginning at my feet and moving to my face.

My mind wanders.

***

The latch releases, setting free a multitude of fellow Homo sapiens as they exit the room, each on a shared journey to have their minds wiped clean once more, preparing for the challenges of the upcoming day.

But somehow, I can remember everything. I am immune to the liquid, to the drugs – to everything. We are all just one hidden experiment.

What happens when we fall asleep? When the mind is blank, when the world is blank – what happens?

This liquid stops our mind from thinking, it stops everything – because somehow, we were all trapped in this experiment that no one can remember.

What is this liquid?

Why do they not want us remembering?

Who are they?

MEASURELESS

Blackness.

Exactly how I imagined it.

If I imagined it to be a 'paradise', it would have been exactly that. This is just exactly what you thought it was going to be.

And I thought it was going to be nothing.

When entire conversations exist only within your mind, you blend reality and your thoughts together. And I was constantly forgetting what I had actually vocalised to others - thinking that they could read my mind.

A liability, not an asset.

When I am constantly saying, "sorry", for never remembering if I had *actually* verbalised my answer, people become exasperated.

It is like a never-ending internal monologue.

We spend half of our lives speaking to ourselves – well, most of us anyways, considering not all of us have an inner voice.

I always sit in the corner - my voice helps me not feel as lonely.

"Talisha…

"Talisha

"Talisha! What are you doing?"

Whoops. And there I go. Being a liability. We can't even escape ourselves.

I guess it was always my worst fear - being stuck inside my head for the rest of time. Nothing else to distract me.

When you think deep enough, in this dimension or the next, you are just stuck. Everyone is.

Time is all just a measurement.

And without time, we do not even exist.

We exist so we can become stuck in ourselves.

Two different people exist externally and internally of our bodies. We are all searching for something - our goal being different on the inside and outside. Even after 10 years, I am still that girl in the corner, too afraid to say something that her mind already hasn't. I still have the same, never-ending thoughts that I did in school. What will set me free?

In this never-ending spiral of ourselves, where do we run to?

The younger version of our self that was still afraid?

In this blackness, I can still feel the presence of my body...just floating.

Even if I try to open my eyes, darkness appears. I try to rub the feeling away whenever it happens and continue to just keep my eyes shut.

I am finally alone.

Stuck in my own head.

A never-ending process of my thoughts.

"Talisha

"Talisha…

"Talisha, are you okay? Everyone is stuck here. Help us."

Throughout time, we are stuck. We become measureless. We are stuck alone with our thoughts. Stuck.

AFTERLIFE?

It's a common mystery, isn't it? The 'afterlife'. And maybe it is meant to be left as a universal mystery – where do we go once we perish, do we even die, is this just the beginning of our life? I think it's nice that every single person experiences the universal truth of death, and it connects us. We all know death. It is the great equaliser of the world. And, of course, there are so many theories of what it *could* be…

1. My main theory:
    -   That the afterlife will consist of whatever image, video – whatever - you have conjured in your mind to be. Whichever way you believed heaven or hell to resemble (or something else entirely, like a whole other world), it will look exactly how you pictured it. For me, I feel like it will be a similar experience to how we sleep. Pitch black. And we won't actually ever know that we've died. Like sleep, you don't know that you've fallen asleep until you wake up. So,

you won't know that you're dead because you will never wake up.

2. My theory part 2:
    -   Earth is just a stepping stone into the next place. And death is the gateway into the next world. Although life is the longest thing that we will ever do, it is also way too short in comparison to the timeline of the world. Surely, this is all part of one big experiment that someone is conducting somewhere and needs a select few of us to continue it?

3. Religious theories:
    -   There are various different theories about death according to different religions. In most of them, heaven and hell exist and allow you to think about your actions and where it will lead you. Predeterminism is evident in some cases, as well as karma. Some believe that their spirit returns to God, with the body becoming dust and the soul no longer existing.

4. Omniscient theory:
    -   There are many theories that people have where they believe that their loved ones can watch over them. Like an omniscient point of view – able to watch anything at any time but not able to interact. It is as if they're floating above us and stuck in our time forever, watching from above.

5. Scientific theory:
    -   And then there is the scientific theory of death, with death being described clearly as when the heart stops beating and the brain and body shut down completely. Your body decomposes and you wonder how this has even changed when you were just alive? When there was a living thing inside. Which

reinforces the metaphysical and arbitrary concept espoused by people who believe in spiritual harmony of a soul. People that fear the unknown and the inability to understand a world outside our own.

And so, if we actually *knew* what will happen after death, would we act any differently? If we knew how we died, would we act any differently? Would we be more careless or not waste a second? Would we continue with our same habits or change something if it was the cause?

After this, we ask, why are we all honestly here then?

To simply experience death together or how our perception shapes how we experience death? And you wonder why there has been left such a large *gap* and elephant in our society. With death constantly tolling over us daily.

And then we reflect upon time and how death is dependent upon time, with time only being a measurement created by humans. So, without time, we don't exist.

Would *you* change who you are if this universal gap was filled?

WE ARE NECESSARY

God started with chaos. A shining light blaring in his imagination - and so does the good. God created humanity. A single howl grappling towards the beauty of nature - the good needing to restore this. God watches his production. Slowly becoming fragile through our unfathomable actions - the good needing to finally outbalance the evil.

It is a simple 'flick' of an action. A barrier between restoration and freedom.

It seems easy; helping a stranger with their groceries, picking up rubbish that isn't yours or letting a car in front of you while driving.

Imagine...just imagine...that you walk past an elderly lady, attempting to transfer their groceries to their car. And you see the problem - but continue to walk past. And again, your unfathomable stream of thoughts activates and you think, "oh, that isn't my problem, the next person will do something".

What if every person after you thinks the same thing? And by the time someone does something about this, the world is already destroyed. And the balance of evil that God created is too overpowering.

You can't have Earth on 'life support' because they support all life. You can't burn the ladder you stand on. You can't burn the wings that support you in flying. This ends with everyone having no life and no support. This, this, is hell. And the evil is beginning to outweigh the good.

The shining light becomes a void. The clear vision becomes a fog left in history. The actions become meaningless.

A single conscious decision to avoid petrol, to avoid coal, and gas and plastic and waste. Our world has given us life. And no matter how much we try to destroy ourselves, our meaning…our worth…cannot be destroyed.

WHY AM I NOT LIKE THEM?

For her? They were the 'cool' ones stereotypically. And she knew that she could never be them, but why?

Was it because of how much 'trouble' they got into? When really it amounted to nothing. Was it because of how low their grades were? But marks shouldn't matter this much. Was it because she herself was intimidated by people like them and swore to never make someone feel the way the 'cool' girls did in her year? She wasn't bullied though and wasn't intimidated easily. Was it because she saw how much words destroyed the lives of people around her from the 'popular' girls at school? Yeah. She cared too much about other people. Maybe the key difference was that she cared for others in a way that they never could. Maybe it was because she always took things way too seriously from such a young age. Maybe it was because she wanted to always include everyone and make everyone comfortable being in their own skin.

What made them popular? What made them cool? Not all pretty girls were in these groups. Not all of them were mean. Other people had good fashion sense. So, what actually defined them as popular or cool? Was it the way they treated other people? Was it their outgoing personalities? What was it?

I still do not know to this day.

ECHOES OF THE ABYSS

In the twilight's silent embrace,

Where shadows dance and memories trace.

As you stare out into the abyss,

You ponder the moments that you've missed.

A tapestry of time unwinds,

Threads of joy and sorrow it binds.

The echoes of laughter and tears,

Whispering through the passing years.

In the canvas of the cosmic night,

Stars illuminate the path so bright.

Each twinkle, a story to tell,

Of triumphs, defeats, and moments to dwell.

The constellations paint tales untold,

Of adventures and mysteries, bold.

Through the vastness, your mind does soar,

Exploring the cosmos, seeking something more.

In the silence, where thoughts collide,

The universe as your guide.

You question the choices made,

In the symphony of life, your part played.

The abyss, a mirror reflecting back,

The journey, the courage, the wisdom you lack.

Yet, in the stillness, you find your way,

A new chapter dawns, a brand-new day.

So, embrace the unknown, fearless and free,

For the future unfolds, a tapestry.

In the vastness, where dreams persist,

Discover the wonders you once dismissed.

OUR DEFINITION OF THE UNKNOWN

How would our perception and definition of femininity and masculinity change if the stereotypical roles and features swapped? What actually makes a face look feminine and what makes it masculine? Is it the depth of our voices or the gentle softness of energy? Long hair, long eyelashes, long nails – why is this considered feminine? Or is it the behaviours, expectations and societal roles that build these ideas?

What if these features were swapped? Would our definition of femininity and masculinity swap, or would these words follow with the features currently associated? What are the foundational layers to what is considered masculine and feminine?

LIFE IS <u>TIME</u>

NO LIGHTS IN TIME

This world never stops.

It is hollow and empty and we are all alone inside.

Life is a metaphor.

And we are all components of this statement.

If we stopped, what would happen?

Time would continue - obviously - but the world would stop. And it would still continue. The natural aspects of the universe would still occur, but everything inside would end.

Would something else in the universe continue and take our place?

No lights can turn out the dark.

What keeps us all awake at night?
Our brains are itinerant. They never terminate.
And neither will time.

***

As my mind wanders, my body begins to wander too.

At midnight, lifting the pure white sheets off my body. My eyes shut, but my brain is still wide awake. Walking out of the house, past the streetlights, house lights, car lights. Past any form of light. Even the light in myself.

Whispers.

Whispers from voices I knew were directing me where to go. Extending my arm, trying to grab these voices as if they were real. The voices are clear. But I could not understand what they were saying. I could not understand anything.

These whispers lead me to a street. A street with no lights, no houses and no cars. Abandoned.

Pitch black.

No lights can turn out the dark.

I stand there, gasping for air, trying to find where I was and where I had been. I am lost.

Not physically.

But lost in myself.

I brought myself here.

Why?

And someone arrives.

I am afraid.

Because I am afraid of myself.

No lights *could* turn out the dark.

The dark within, and the dark within the world.

I see myself, standing.

No expression, no emotions, no feelings.

Just…standing…there.

The figure slightly fades into the background, with a vast tinge of blackness covering it. I could not see my eyes, ears, nose or mouth, but I knew it was me.

The figure leisurely comes closer, and in an instant, a flash of my entire life comes.

Everything I had lost.

Every regret, every opportunity, every failure. Every memory I had lost.

It all came back.

The figure takes another step closer, "What do you want?"

I did not want anything.

I had searched for myself.

And I lost a part of myself in time.

I reached out, to try and touch the figure. I relied on touching objects to see if they were real. But I already knew that this moment was real.

All I wanted was to see what I used to be.

To remember who I used to be.

But I did not want anything from myself.

All I wanted was to see how much of myself I had lost throughout time.

I am afraid of myself and what I turned into.

No lights could turn out the dark of my own shadow.

Your own psyche.

No lights could turn out what is inside your mind.

***

Why does your mind want to bring your body pain?

You spend your entire life inside your mind and all it creates is physical pain.

***

I am struggling.

Her face is imprinted in my mind, forever.

My body begins to move, one foot in front of the other. One movement in front of the other.

My body takes me out of my house, at midnight, and I continue to move - my feet being the only sound resonating in me.

My eyes are closed, my mind is awake and my consciousness is breathing in the universe.

I see visions.

Visions inside my mind.

Visions that are clearly there, but I cannot grasp it - I just cannot reach them.

My body continues to move, with visions of silhouetted humans in my mind. One face becomes clear.

A face that I had hoped I would never remember. And yet I remembered her every day.

Her face is in my mind. It is stuck in my psyche.

And as my eyes opened, my body had brought me to a store that was abandoned. There was no form of light.

It is pitch black. No lights can turn out the dark.

How did I get here?

Sharp, stabbing ringing overpowered my ears and I stood still. Waiting for the moment to pass.

Every other noise in the world went blank. The world went blank. All I focused on were the words that my mind was putting into focus.

Words that person had killed me with.

Sounds were the only thing that had destroyed me, and they continue to destroy me now.

Flashes of her words went through my brain.

In my mind, I had searched for the sounds that changed me. To repeat them in my mind again, and again.

I could not see anything, everything was blank, but all I could hear was her voice repeating those words.

"You destroyed my life."

I am suffocating inside my own mind.

Every day, sound is what destroys me.

No lights could turn out the dark of my own shadow.

Sound is what destroys you.
You focus on the noise in the world.
But noise is what *created* you.
You should be more afraid of yourself.

***

You are afraid of the world.

Of your own psyche, what is inside of you - what you are made of.

Why?

You are your own psyche.

***

I am alone.

I have become damaged by my own mind.

I do not even feel connected to myself anymore.

At midnight, I feel my body lift into the air and begin to walk out of the door in my room. My eyes cannot open. I am trying to see where my body is taking me, but it hurts every time I flinch my eye.

I am stuck in the dark.

My body walks out of my house and down the streets to somewhere. I do not know where I am going. I can not recognise the smells or the feel of the ground against my feet. My body continues to walk.

I feel my body walk past any form of darkness.

Bright visions begin to fill the outside of my eyes.

Everything around me is beaming with light.

Vivid, blazing, intense glows begin to fill my eyes.

No lights can turn out the dark.

There is too much dark within me, and I have always tried to cover it up with visuals.

I am afraid to open my eyes, to see what is covered behind a closed eyelid.

I have been hiding my entire life.

And now I am hiding from myself.

Why?

I am scared to reveal the truth and to stop hiding from myself and from everyone else. I am scared of the world. I always have been.

No lights could turn out the dark of my own shadow.

Are you afraid to see your true self?

Do not hide away from me, I am a reflection of you.

I am your body.

I am your soul.

I am your mind.

Do not be afraid.

***

You have robbed yourself from humanity. Every person sees their own mind and shadow, but they all treat the situation differently.

Humans are daunted by their senses, their own mind and being alone.

You become vulnerable when you experience all three feelings.

And that is when shadows twist you, and destroy you.

No light *can* destroy us, but the only light that can, is the light inside of your mind. You summoned us. You made us real in *your* world.

117

Each person that has met their shadow had to travel inside of their own mind to meet that shadow when they were unconscious.

You are terrified of yourself.

You have met your mind.

You have met the substantial trigger inside your mind.

This is what makes your brain tick. What makes you go.

It means everything.

If humans stopped, shadows would take over.

If shadows stopped, what would happen?

Would time continue?

We keep all of you awake at night.

You have no power against us.

But what is a shadow?

A shadow is you.

You are a shadow.

★ ★ ★

HOME

Soul mates? They exist. Of course they do. But not always romantically and not always a human.

It's a friend that brings you an immediate safe space wherever you go. It's a pet where you feel like you can speak to them and they can understand you. It is a situation where you're afraid and a person allows you to be yourself. It's your dog where you would feel absolutely lost without them as they are always there for you. It's the place where you live and the people there that makes you the happiest you have ever been – despite all of the hurdles. It's home.

Soul mates? They're like this home.

Where no matter where you go, these certain things will connect more with you than anyone else. Where these certain things make you present. Where these certain things make you feel like the universe isn't all that big.

A CHOICE?

There comes a point in your life where you finally wake up to the reality of everything. Where you see everyone else's lives come together and yours begins to fall apart. When the mountain of worries, fears and disruptions continue to pile up on one another.

People have always told me, 'You're so strong,' 'You're so resilient,' 'You'll get through it'.

But the truth is, I was never given a choice.

And absolutely everyone goes through or will go through something difficult in their lives and you will never be able to compare it to someone else. But what you hope that you can find in someone, is that they care enough to try. Someone cares enough to understand your feelings, because no matter how much they listen they will never be able to fully understand or relate to your specific pain.

But it's not just pain.

It's everything.

It's being confused and feeling different your entire life.

It's begging to feel somewhat 'normal' and for others to finally understand that you're not.

It's continually asking, 'Why me,' and, 'Why not me'?

It's asking if my dream will even be possible in the future when I struggle to get through every day?

It's being forced to accept the hand you have been given because you have absolutely no choice.

It's being afraid to pass this onto future generations.

It's everything.

RED DOOR

The final strides echoed with urgency. "We must return; I made a promise," he declared, locking eyes with her, a glimmer of hope shared between them. The gravity of their quest held them captive as they approached the ominous red door, sealing their destiny in its brilliance.

A mirrored reflection greeted them, reminiscent of their parents frozen in time. "We'll find them. I swear it," his determination whispered, a pledge heavy with the weight of the past. The same fateful promise that once condemned their parents now echoed through the corridor of time, ensuring their own entanglement in a web of destiny. The door, though identical in its rusted elegance, retained its haunting allure – a portal that beckoned, a passage to the unknown.

Twelve years had passed since that portal first opened, swallowing their parents into a pool of uncertainty. Twelve years of tireless pursuit, and now, standing before it again, the door mocked them with its silence, as if time itself had halted within its confines. The same rusted cogs turned, the clocks remained devoid of numbers, and the red hue, a vivid scarlet echo of the past, promised both salvation and doom.

Their hands pressed against the solid oak, feeling the weight of years etched into its surface. The door yielded slowly to their touch, a gateway to a realm where the echoes of their parents' disappearance lingered. The blinding light enveloped them, and the unfolding events seemed eerily familiar to any onlooker. History, it appeared, had chosen to repeat itself.

Yet, within the crimson glow, an altered reality unfolded. They weren't entrapped in the same door that had claimed their parents; instead, they found themselves thrust into the vivid memories of their parents' lives. The passage of time became fluid, as they were drawn into a poignant journey, reliving the moments that had shaped the destiny of those who had vanished before them. The red door, once a gateway to uncertainty, now revealed itself as a conduit to understanding, as they traversed the labyrinth of their parents' existence, determined to unearth the secrets that had eluded them for twelve long years.

LEARNING

I'm learning to say no, without feeling guilty.

I'm learning to prioritise myself, without explaining it to others.

I'm learning to be myself, without begging to be someone else.

I'm learning to forgive others, for my own closure.

I'm learning to be kind to myself, perfection is an illusion.

I'm learning that uncertainty is OK, with the unknown.

I'm learning to be grateful, and do good with what I'm given.

I'm learning not to be jealous of others, and focus on myself.

I'm learning that is OK to be lost, without blaming myself.

I'm learning to continue learning, without fear for what I do not know.

★ ★ ★

THE COLOUR OF OPTIMISM

If you were limited to only seeing one colour for the rest of your life, what would you choose? Would it be the colour of red or the colour of blue? The colour of an emotion? Of optimism? How would you choose to see the world?

In a world painted in the hues of optimism, every sunrise would be a canvas of golden promises, a symphony of hope cascading across the horizon. The colour of optimism would be a warm, inviting shade, like the gentle glow of a candle flickering in the darkness, promising that even in the face of adversity, there is always light.

Imagine a world where every act of kindness, every selfless gesture, is bathed in the gentle radiance of this optimistic colour. It would be a world where compassion and empathy shine through, where the beauty of human connections is shown by the vibrant tones of understanding.

The colour of optimism would transform the mundane into the extraordinary. A simple walk in the park would become a journey through a lush tapestry of greens and pinks, as the colour reflects the beauty in every leaf and flower. The air would be tinged with the hope for our future.

In this world, setbacks and challenges would be seen not as obstacles but as opportunities painted in the rich palette of resilience. The colour of optimism would infuse every setback with a touch of vibrancy, turning moments of difficulty into stepping stones toward personal growth and success.

Relationships, too, would be illuminated by the colour of optimism. Every shared smile, every hug, and every word of encouragement would be highlighted by the brilliance of this colour, creating a kaleidoscope of love and support that binds people together.

The colour of optimism would be a constant reminder that, despite the shadows that may fall, there is always a spectrum of possibilities waiting to be explored. It would be a beacon of light guiding you through the twists and turns of life, encouraging you to see challenges not as insurmountable barriers, but as opportunities for growth and learning.

So, if you could only see one more colour for the rest of your life, perhaps the colour of optimism would be the choice that paints your world with the brushstrokes of endless possibilities and unwavering hope.

How would you choose to see the world?

ECHO OF TIME

In the realm of the now, transformed and vast,

A shadow reflects, questions from the past.

Intricacies woven, life's intricate lace,

Echoes of a journey, in time's embrace.

Do you dance in the storm, or watch from afar?

A silent wish maker, or the bright guiding star?

Is your canvas painted in vibrant hues?

Or do you wander, in a maze of subdued views?

A spectre of change, in the mirror's gaze,

Whispers of a past, in the future's maze.

An enigma, this dance of light and shade,

A fleeting waltz, in the hours unmade.

In the flux of time, a lingering fear,

Of lost echoes, faint yet clear.

Is the essence fading, in time's swift stream?

Or growing stronger, in the silent dream?

A cryptic message, from then to now,

In the unfolding story, a silent vow.

A journey through time's mysterious door,

Seeking truths, hidden in the core.

LIFE IS ___

Life is hard. Life is unfair. Life is extraordinary. Life is weird. Life is magical. Life is awful. Life is your perception. Life is relaxing. Life is serious. Life is a joke. Life is dull. Life is yours. Life is stupid. Life is challenging. Life is unusual. Life is purposeful. Life is humbling. Life is chaotic. Life is easy. Life is short. Life is long. Life is mysterious. Life is universal. Life is harsh. Life is subjective. Life is unknown. Life is hard-work. Life is charming. Life is worthwhile. Life is authentic. Life is a measurement. Life is based on time. Life is beautiful. Life is sincere. Life is delightful. Life is fulfilling. Life is two-faced. Life is fighting. Life is deep. Life is shallow. Life is natural. Life is death. Life is full of memories. Life is living. Life is motion. Life is happy. Life is sad. Life is vivid. Life is honest. Life is heartless. Life is bright. Life is full of change. Life is cheerful. Life is creative. Life is full of dreams. Life is good. Life is growth. Life is honourable. Life is lifeless. Life is peaceful. Life is playful. Life is real. Life is quiet. Life is rewarding. Life is rich. Life is surprising. Life is uncommon. Life is wonderous. Life is amazing. Life is blissful. Life is breathtaking. Life is complex. Life is full of change. Life is dynamic. Life is enchanting. Life is euphoric. Life is evolving. Life is expansive. Life is gorgeous. Life is graceful. Life is healing. Life is full of hope. Life is inspiring. Life is illuminating. Life is abrasive. Life is inhumane. Life is full of love. Life is gentle. Life is full of hate. Life is mesmerising. Life is aggressive. Life is pleasant. Life is mortality. Life is missing. Life is rich. Life is witty. Life is resilient. Life is thrilling. Life is bad. Life is good. Life is unique. Life is vibrant. Life is zealous. Life is youthful. Life is brutal. Life is bitter. Life is incredible. Life is twisted. Life is sensational. Life is disappointing. Life is awesome. Life is overwhelming. Life is tiring. Life is confusing. Life is taken-for-granted. Life is constant. Life is discovery. Life is ecstatic. Life is painful. Life is horrible. Life is dazzling. Life is transcendent. Life is underappreciated. Life is passionate. Life is spiritual. Life is fluid. Life is simple. Life is tomorrow. Life is yesterday. Life is the present. Life could be better. Life could be worse. Life is crazy. Life is your imagination. Life is experiences. Life is appreciation. Life is what we see. Life is responsibility. Life is focusing. Life is energy. Life is like a movie. Life is a gift. Life is a story. Life is holding on. Life is transformative. Life is the past. Life is your past. Life is the future. Life is unforgettable.

You know what life is?

Life is just the experiences you have between the two times you are dead. Before you are born and after.

And maybe this whole experience is not meant to be described.

THANK YOU!

There are so many people that have helped me write this book but I would have to write another book if I thanked them all.

I want to thank two people in particular. Kim Allen has been an inspiration to me and has always been very supportive of my writing endeavours. As with my first book, Kim also read the first draft of this book and gave me a number of areas to fine tune. Thank you, Kim. I appreciate your hard work and I hope you are proud of the final copy!

This book also contains not just my imagination and dreams but also the unwavering support and guidance from my father. His patience, wisdom, and encouragement were only matched by the practical help in laying out this book and preparing it for print. He has been the invisible ink, if you like, to bring my words to you. Thanks Dad, your belief in me has been the greatest gift of all.

ABOUT THE AUTHOR

Julia Dickerson, at just twenty years of age, has completed her second book, "Life is ___", a compelling collection of forty short stories in a dystopian genre. This work, ingeniously segmented into five categories - Fighting, Memories, Perceptions, Unknown and Time - echoes a profound and consistent message: life throws many obstacles, but one should never compromise their true self.

Jules began her storytelling journey with her first published book at the age of fifteen in 2019. Now, five years later, she has grown significantly as a writer. Her passion for English and creative writing has always been the driving force behind her writing, receiving numerous awards throughout her academic and personal life.

"Life is ___" is not just a testament to her growth as a writer, it is an invitation for readers to explore their perceptions of reality. Jules challenges and changes conventional thinking through each story, whilst pushing the boundaries of what a story should be.

This book is a big step in her journey as a writer, showing her unique style and how she sees the world.

Having navigated the challenges and triumphs of life herself, Jules hopes to continue to inspire and challenge her readers, one story at a time.

Her debut book, "Stopping Time", is available on Amazon as a paperback or eBook.